# SADIE SPROCKET
## Builds a ROCKET

By Sue Fliess • Illustrated by Annabel Tempest

two lions

Published by Two Lions, New York

www.apub.com

Amazon, the Amazon logo, and Two Lions are trademarks of
Amazon.com, Inc., or its affiliates.

ISBN-13: 9781542018036 (hardcover)
ISBN-10: 154201803X (hardcover)

The illustrations are rendered in digital media.

Book design by Tanya Ross-Hughes

Printed in China

First Edition

10 9 8 7 6 5 4 3 2 1

To Dr. Maggie Aderin-Pocock, for
inspiring kids—especially girls—of all races
to pursue science. Let's get you to Mars!
—S. F.

For my goddaughter Bumble Ayres,
who I love to Mars and back!
—A. T.

**Sadie Sprocket** had a wish
to travel far from here,
to venture through the galaxy
beyond our atmosphere.

She checked out every book on space,
learned all there was to know.
"No one's been to Mars," she said.
"I'll be the first to go!"

So one day Sadie drew a map
to navigate the stars.
"It's time to leave the Earth," she said,
"and travel straight to Mars!"

Because the journey would be long,
she thought she'd bring a crew.

She interviewed and tested each,
and then she chose a few.

"First we need to build a ship
that's sturdy, safe, and fast.
To make it there without a hitch,
it must be built to last."

They rummaged through the junkyard
and gathered every part.

They counted, weighed, and measured twice.
She couldn't wait to start.

Sadie and her crew worked hard
to build her rocket ship.
She scanned her map and chose a date
to make the stellar trip.

"We launch today!" young Sadie said.
"I've tested every switch."
She knew that even one small blip
could cause a major glitch.

Friends and family wished her well.
Reporters flocked to see . . .
This space-bound girl with smarts and skill
would soon make history.

"Ten,
nine,
eight!"

she counted down.
The engine shook the lawn.

"Seven,
six,
five,
four,
three,
two—

and ONE!"

The ship was gone!

The journey took one hundred days!
She knew it would be tough.
But Sadie kept their spirits up.
**"We'll be there soon enough!"**

The crew tried playing cards and games without too much success.
The pieces floated all around and made an awful mess!

Instead, they read to pass the time
and took turns making food . . .
while Sadie wrote down everything
and tracked their altitude.

The Earth behind, so far away,
was now a tiny dot.
Then Sadie cried, "There's planet Mars!
It's smaller than I thought!"

As their ship was closing in,
the captain told her crew,
"We'll set up camp and gather samples.
We've got work to do!"

Sadie scanned her map of Mars
and found a place to land.
"We'll put the ship down over there,
upon the level sand."

"Get your samples," Sadie said.
They filled up twenty bags.

They tied them tight and labeled them,
and then they planted flags.

After one last photograph,
they packed up their supplies.
Then Sadie stopped to look around . . .
and noticed flashing skies.

"A storm is coming. Time to go!"
They strapped in for the flight.
But then the rocket wouldn't budge.
They couldn't leave the site!

"The landing gear is buried deep!
We have to dig it free."

They jumped back in,
but sand was swirling . . .
Now they couldn't see!

When the storm had settled down,
they got their chance to fly.
But then the rocket wouldn't start!

"There's one thing left to try."

She quickly grabbed her rocket tools
and checked the circuit board.

They cleared the sand

and fixed the wires . . .
Power was restored!

Once the ship had warmed enough,
she shouted, "Time to blast!"
They zoomed by stars and asteroids
and made it home, at last.

Sadie made the nightly news.
The world now knew her name.
The first to land on planet Mars
had rocketed to fame.

She'd triumphed in her mission.
But Sadie wasn't done.

This pioneer of space had plans . . .
She'd only just begun.

"One more question, please," they said.
"What's next for you, Miss Sprocket?"

"Maybe Neptune, but for that,
I'll need a bigger rocket."

# SADIE'S NOTEBOOK

## ALL ABOUT MARS

- Mars is called "the red planet" because its surface contains a lot of iron oxide, or rust, giving it a reddish color. This may make Mars look hot, but most of the time, it's freezing cold. Its thin atmosphere allows heat to bounce back into space. It can get up to 75 degrees Farenheit (24°C) during the day and as low as –166 degrees Farenheit (–110°C) at night.

- Mars is the fourth planet from the sun. It is about half the size of Earth. Like Earth, it is a rocky planet with valleys and volcanoes. It has four seasons, but its seasons are twice as long as the seasons on Earth.

- The tallest mountain in the solar system is on Mars. It's called the Olympus Mons and is 15.4 miles (24.8 km) high—three times higher than Mount Everest!

- Mars also has a canyon that is more than five times as deep as the Grand Canyon. It would stretch from New York to San Francisco.

- Scientists have discovered water on Mars, but they're still trying to figure out if there is life inside these salty streams. NASA has sent robotic explorers to Mars, and it is now developing the capabilities needed to send humans to the red planet sometime in the 2030s!

## ALL ABOUT WOMEN IN SPACE

- Caroline Herschel (1750-1848) discovered her first comet on August 1, 1786. She was the first woman to be recognized for discovering a comet and went on to discover eight more!

- As a student of astronomy, Annie Jump Cannon (1863-1941) devised a classification system for stars based on their temperatures.

- The first female astronaut was a Russian named Valentina Tereshkova (1937-). In 1963, she was the first and youngest woman to have flown in space on a solo mission. It would be twenty more years before the United States sent a woman into space.

- Sally Ride (1951-2012) was the youngest and first American female astronaut to go to space. She traveled with four other astronauts on the *Challenger* space shuttle.

- Astronomer Nancy Grace Roman (1925-2018) is known to many as the "Mother of the Hubble" because she helped develop the Hubble Space Telescope. She discovered that stars with different compositions followed different orbits around the galaxy. Her results led to a better understanding of the structure of our Milky Way galaxy.

- Astronomer and professor Andrea Ghez (1965-) is considered one of the top twenty scientists in the United States. She researches black holes and discovered a massive one in our galaxy. She is working to solve the mystery of how the universe was formed.

- Maggie Aderin-Pocock (1968-), a PhD in physics, helped create a satellite system for monitoring the earth's atmosphere. One of her dreams is to fly to Mars.